Raffi Songs to Read®

If You're Happy and You Know It

Adapted by Raffi
Illustrated by Cyd Moore

Alfred A. Knopf   New York

For Lindsay and Branden, who bring me much happiness!—C.M.

THIS IS A BORZOI BOOK PUBLISHED BY ALFRED A. KNOPF
Text copyright © 2001 by Homeland Publishing (SOCAN). Traditional; new verse by Raffi.
Illustrations copyright © 2005 by Cyd Moore
Front cover photograph copyright © Colin Goldie, GM Studios
Back cover photograph copyright © 2004 by Carrie Nuttall
All rights reserved under International and Pan-American Copyright Conventions.
Published in the United States of America by Alfred A. Knopf, an imprint of
Random House Children's Books, a division of Random House, Inc., New York,
and simultaneously in Canada by Random House of Canada Limited, Toronto.
Distributed by Random House, Inc., New York.

www.randomhouse.com/kids

RAFFI SONGS TO READ and SONGS TO READ are registered trademarks of Troubadour Learning,
a division of Troubadour Records Ltd.
KNOPF, BORZOI BOOKS, and the colophon are registered trademarks of
Random House, Inc.

Library of Congress Cataloging-in-Publication Data
Raffi.
If you're happy and you know it / adapted by Raffi ; illustrated by Cyd Moore.
p. cm. — (Raffi songs to read)
SUMMARY: An illustrated version of the famous song that asks readers to clap their hands.
ISBN 0-375-82917-2 (trade) — ISBN 0-375-92917-7 (lib. bdg.)
1. Children's songs—Texts. [1. Songs.] I. Title: If you are happy and you know it. II. Moore, Cyd, ill.
III. Title. IV. Series: Raffi. Raffi songs to read.
PZ8.3.R124 If 2005
782.42—dc22
2004010312

Printed in the United States of America
November 2005
10 9 8 7 6 5 4 3 2 1
First Edition

. . . let it ring: *ding-a-ling-ling*.

If you're bananas and you know it,
let it ring: *ding-a-ling-ling*.

If you're bananas and you know it,
and you really wanna show it—

If you're beautiful and you know it,
and you really wanna show it—

If you're beautiful and you know it,
shout "Hooray!"

If you're beautiful and you know it,
shout "Hooray!"

. . . shout "Hooray!"

If you're beautiful and you know it,

If you're bananas and you know it,
let it ring: *ding-a-ling-ling*.

If You're Happy and You Know It

traditional: adapted by Raffi

If you're hap-py and you know it, clap your hands. If you're hap-py and you know it, clap your hands. If you're hap-py and you know it, and you real-ly wan-na show it—If you're hap-py and you know it, clap your hands!

If you're bananas and you know it,
  let it ring: *ding-a-ling-ling.*
If you're bananas and you know it,
  let it ring: *ding-a-ling-ling.*
If you're bananas and you know it,
  and you really wanna show it—
If you're bananas and you know it,
  let it ring: *ding-a-ling-ling.*

If you're beautiful and you know it,
  shout "Hooray!"
If you're beautiful and you know it,
  shout "Hooray!"
If you're beautiful and you know it,
  and you really wanna show it—
If you're beautiful and you know it,
  shout "Hooray!"

If you're happy and you know it,
  clap your hands.
If you're happy and you know it,
  clap your hands.
If you're happy and you know it,
  and you really wanna show it—
If you're happy and you know it,
  clap your hands!